Batey Descending

Batey

Nico Pengin

Published by NicoPengin.com, 2021.

While every precaution has been taken in the preparation of this book, the publisher assumes no responsibility for errors or omissions, or for damages resulting from the use of the information contained herein.

BATEY DESCENDING

First edition. September 30, 2021.

ISBN: 979-8201007843

Written by Nico Pengin.

Also by Nico Pengin

Batey
Batey Ascending
Batey Descending

Batey - Español
Batey Ascendiendo

Standalone
la Insurrección de los Lápices
Uprising of the Pencils: Revised Edition
Batey

Watch for more at https://nicopengin.com/.

Table of Contents

To my sister, ImCompletelyMe, I love you, just not the memories of getting beat up before I could develop muscles. Enjoy this what if story inspired by you :)

CHAPTER 1

Chilly.

Things don't change in people. When they move, their routines change, but only because they want things to stay the same. On Earth and on Gibraltar, people strive for what makes them feel like things are the same. We work because we want to. We play because we can. Even though the conditions are different, men will still look at me like a fine slice of traveling steak.

Becoming a professional Batey player hasn't changed me much. I'm still me, and I earn the name Chilly, consistently. I have suitors, men and boys alike. All ages and all backgrounds, sticking around me like they're living through a blizzard. All because I give them nothing but the coldest part of my shoulder. None of them are good enough for me; none of them are right.

Even with the Earth in balance and humanity divided, people are still the same. They are so desperate to stay the same because changing that much leads to too many problems. I know that because I've been through that, and I tried to change, and it didn't work.

Just walking into the venue makes me feel that. The surrounding cold. There's no "sky" above us, just illumination that mimics our old, lost sunlight. There are clouds, but they are made out of steam and other produced gases inside this spaceship. It's blue, but it's too shallow. The sky is closer than it used to be. Even though it's supposed to be the "same". It changed, and nobody has any acknowledgement of it. I haven't met one person who admitted that the sky here is the same or better than the sky on Earth.

So why even choose it? Why do people not change? I wonder why. Maybe they have hope, and I can't sympathize with that issue. Men have hope of warming me up, getting close to me and working their way into my heart, but that's not happening. Not again. Maybe they have hope that they'll feel so good they'll forget where they are.

It won't change the facts.

We're all stuck up here in this alien habitat. Most people see the massive spaceship, Gibraltar, as salvation. But not enough think of it the correct way. It's a prison. That's the real fact, the hard line. The Blues, the aliens that put us in Gibraltar, are keeping us here, making us think they've lifted us up and "saved" us. Its pure superiority at work. A dogma. A system where the weak are celebrated, so the strong can rule them easier. I'm not into it, and I'm astonished that so many are.

All the way into the stadium, up the rows of lights where the New Batey field is stationed. Awaits the first big game of our career as a team. I can feel the heat on me. If I weren't so cold, I'd melt with everyone else. If I weren't Chilly, maybe I'd be Happy, but I'd also be Dumb, just like Nico, my annoying but lovable, little brother.

It's a miracle we ever met at all. After so many years of being disconnected. I still remember getting in trouble, almost daily.

And all the trauma we both went through when we had our lives back on Earth. I was five years ahead of him. Somehow, that was enough to turn him into some hopeful, deceived, and gullible boy. While I stayed strong, independent, and furious at the truth that my eyes and ears witnessed.

We're ready to play. They call out my name, and I run into the field, and that's the first and last time that I listen to someone telling me what to do. I work with the team because the team works with me, not the other way around. They trust me to take care of my positions, so I do. They trust me so I can deliver results. They trust me, and sometimes, I wish they didn't. Because I still can't trust any of them.

The feeling is not mutual.

Gorri is on the backline, playing the goalkeeper. Not surprised. The old man has loved to be the director of the defense, ever since I met him. He needs to look the strongest even when he's weak. That must have been how he lived before. He's all our senior; he was still an adult when the spaceship came by. He probably had a family, and they probably hated him. No one likes to be consistently bossed around like that. He gives off a family man vibe.

Yuck.

It's us or nothing now. The game keeps going on. Nico's surprisingly fast. He's brave and strong for his size. He grew up well, not that I helped make that happen much. I left so soon, and then the Blues came down. And while I waited to head up, bide my time and make a plan for my future, he just went along with it. He ran away from home like I did. Of all the things to influence, maybe I gave him the wrong ideas.

These players on the other team, the RTG boys, hit hard. They aren't afraid to treat a delicate and gentle lady rough. Not like all the other men. The ones who buy me whatever I want, give me Cred whenever I ask, never backing down from my selfish requests. A word was created for men like that. The ones who treat women like they're the most precious thing to ever come into space, just for them and no one else. Society calls them simps. I call them simpletons.

None of these boys fall for me, though. They'd sooner punch me than ask me out to dinner. At least they're professional about it. I've got nothing to give them except my best effort. A few kicks for good luck. And that's a hard-fought battle.

The big one charges at me, as wide as he is tall. If I asked him about it, he'd probably call it "muscular fat." Well, I have a karate fist, all muscle and bone, so I check him right into the softest part of his pads. He moves; I don't. That's a lifetime of training. A technique forged through millions of repetitions He wouldn't understand.

But another one comes in to snipe me. He's charging in, knees first, on a slide tackle, and he gets taken out before I can even see what happened. I followed the trail down to the bottom of the arena. One went out, and the other jumped right off and rejoined the fight. We're up a player while they're down. Nico was the one who got there that quick.

Who stole the center of attention.

Again.

CHAPTER 2

I used to be Happy. Not my real name, but it's what my parents called me. I was the happiest baby, never crying, even when I should have. Maybe I cried, but it was only until I learned how to laugh. Once I did it, I was smiling all the time for the first five years of my life. And I loved it.

I loved my Mama more than anything at all. She was my world. The earliest memories I have, are of being at home with her while she held me on her lap. She'd roll up the dough and start cooking dinner for Pa in the afternoon. Then she'd put me down for a nap. Singing soft Taino lullaby songs to me, even though I wouldn't understand the words or strange rhythm. Still, it worked so quickly and effectively, and when I woke up, we'd all have a family meal together. The three of us were at our peak of enjoyment together.

I was still happy, even when Pa wasn't. He lost his job when I was still small and didn't know any better about how the world works. I thought it was fun being with him every day, but I could tell just a little that he and Mama weren't doing well. They weren't happy, even though they were together. I didn't understand at the time. How love worked. How people so close, could devastatingly get so far apart.

I didn't understand until Nico was born. That was when my smile was gone for good. It started off slow, with Mama spending all her time with him like she used to do with me. And Pa left again for a new job that lasted a while, so I had no one left. And it was all his fault. He took the center of attention.

MY attention.

I hated him, with all the hate that I could hold in my little five-year-old heart. I didn't know any better. But I knew that things had changed, and I couldn't stand the change. Things were the same for Mama. Except now there were two of us competing for time, love and affection. She'd do all the same things again. Sing him the same songs she sang to me. The weird Taino songs I didn't understand, and preparing dinner with him on her lap like she did with me. Except it was him and not me. Things were the same for her but different for me. I had to survive while my whole life changed and his life didn't. His life had just started, and I was already resenting it.

That's what I thought, anyway. That led me to dark places emotionally in my mind. I started acting out. Pa saw it happening, and Mama couldn't stop it, so he started directing his hate on me. I threw things on the floor, and when that didn't work, I'd ruin dinner—I'd throw it around, I'd scream and holler. I was an unholy terror. I was demanding time, love and affection. I think that it drove my Pa to drink.

I was kicked out of the house during the day when I wasn't at school. They didn't want me in while Nico was there. He was their "Happy" baby now. Not me. Not anymore. Not ever. Instead, they tried to put my anger to use. When I was five, Pa put me in a beginner's karate class to sort through my rage. By the time I was seven, they had given me a black belt.

Piece of piece. Or cake.

The Children's Karate League was easy for me, sure. I was a strong and beautiful girl. Even the trainers had trouble with me because I didn't strive to satisfy them. I threw punches and kicks to hurt them. Because I was strong and wanted to be a pretty and hard - hitting star. I deserved it. It was all about me. All the love, time and attention was fixated on me. The one place I could get all the attention I wanted...

And when I was eight, I was more mellowed out. Our family was still breaking apart, little by little. And I was determined at one point to make it right. Everything started when Mama got pregnant and Pa lost his job. Again. But this time, she lost "it". Her and Pa had to recover from that emotional trauma. I was not so opposed to that predicament. And as Nico came along, it made everything worse, from my own point of view.

He was such a happy and smiling kid. Always full of energy, excitement and curious about the world. He reminded me of myself. I wondered, what do YOU have to be happy about? You're so young, so dumb, and so weak. You don't even know what life is yet. All this. From the mind of an eight-year-old karate black belt holder. Talking down to her toddler brother. In her head.

I snapped one day. I couldn't hold it in. I was so jealous, so hateful. I was so forgotten that I couldn't stand it. It felt like Mama and Pa would never love me again as long as Nico was around. So I knew I had to get rid of him.

The next time our family went shopping. I asked our parents to leave us in the car, so they could enjoy having a shopping date, and they happily agreed. They left us in the car parking lot unsupervised. I thought, if I make him die here. It'll look like we were suffocated, and only he would die and both of my parents would be taken to jail forever! I'll make his death look like an accident, and no one will blame me. I'll get Mama and Pa's attention again. Because he'll be all gone, and they'll only have me, and they will both be punished for not loving **only** me sooner. Then I can be truly happy.

So I tried. I told Nico I'd teach him karate. We did a little punch, he made a little tiny kick, and then I told him a lie. I told him I'd teach him a grappling move. I put his neck into a scissor lock chokehold. Right across his neck. I secured the seatbelt across his mouth and wrapped it around his neck. He couldn't breathe. I was ready to kill him, at least I thought I was. I had no intention of stopping.

But then I was unable to do it. I couldn't do it. I was hateful, vengeful and vile, but I wasn't a murderer...not yet, not to my own flesh and blood. At least not to my own kin. I couldn't kill my own living brother. Hurting was one thing, and it made me feel stronger, but the thought of killing him made me feel sick. I let him go after a few seconds, and the air was heavy with tension.

And then Nico just laughed it off. Once he stopped coughing and dried his eyes from the tears he claimed he had "leaked on reflex", he was laughing it off. "You're really strong, sis," he said. And I was. I was so strong that I got scared. I never really tested myself against someone my own size. I fought with adults for the years that I was practicing, and I was always trying to seriously hurt them. I never realized how weak and fragile kids were.

And I used that strength to my advantage. It gave me the start I needed. Ironically, I was fighting for my place off Earth before the aliens ever even came to us.

CHAPTER 3

The last memories I had of Earth were in the second grade. I was nine years old then. I was put in a place surrounded by kids. I didn't know who I had to pretend were my friends, and although I was young, I knew better. I knew that school was for chumps, especially with a low-income public school like the one I was sent to.

We couldn't afford any better, though. It was that or nothing. Only the worst for baby Chilly. That's around when I started getting called by that name because I'd gotten so cold; everybody knew it. And they made fun of me for it, too. In particular. Three sisters—the Stacks girls—tried their hardest to bring enough heat to melt me down.

Atey Stacks. The wavy-haired one. Nashay Stacks. The curly-haired one. Even though she was only 9, she was already rocking a fake dye. Like a bad weave. And Lilay Stacks. The coily haired one. Who was bigger than the other two, in height and strength. The youngest of the three. I hate the youngest children. I could see their parents through them though. An unloving home that couldn't make time for all of them, so they paid to keep them happy. Rich kids from the hood, aka spoiled brats.

They were brutes and dictators. If they didn't like someone, they did everything they could to get them kicked out of class for some reason. They blamed their own pranks on other kids, whined to get them in trouble, and always had alibis for each other. They had a perfect little racket going on to do whatever they wanted, whenever they wanted. Until they met me.

"Chilly Penguin," they called me. That was the preschool insult that I learned to ignore and never gave them an inch of my mind when they said it. They knew my last name was Pengin, but they would still chant it out.

"Karate Master," was another, sarcastically mocking me for having a sport that I was good at. They did the same to other kids who played during recess, just mocking them for whatever they saw.

"Orphan girl" was the worst one, though. I don't know how they knew or where they heard it, but they found the one thing I couldn't stand. They found out about my family and how abandoned I felt. I never told anyone. It could have been a rumor or a lie, but it hit my soft spot, and they learned about it. Or they just could read my vibe too well.

One day, they circled me while I was getting my things out of my cubby. I just wanted to go home, but not because I missed it there. Home was a place where I could shut myself in my room. I could ignore the surrounding life that I hated, but school wouldn't let me do that. I had to endure it. Hour after hour. Without ever getting a chance to leave like I wanted. And the Stacks girls were the worst part about it.

"Where are you going?",

Atey asked sarcastically.

"She's going to her 'home',"

Nashay remarked,

"under the road, in the sewer, where all the other poop lives."

"She doesn't live in a crap sewer,"

Lilay asserted,

"Her house is much worse than that."

"She has a crappy little baby brother,"

Atey announced. Mocking him didn't budge me at all. I even joined in, in my head.

"I bet her brother,"

Nashay suggested,

"came out of her mama's butt."

Mocking Mama was too far, but not far enough to get me to lash out at them; I wouldn't be blamed for their own ignorant abuse.

"I heard her Papa started drinking,"

Lilay claimed,

"and beat her Mama up for fun."

There are some things even a kid understands are too far to be ignored. But I didn't fight them. I really did not want to. I was too strong for them, and I could kill them if I wanted or if I tried too hard. They caught me glaring at them and surrounded me during recess, in a corner. Away from any teacher's sights. They "tried" pushing me down, but my practice and training paid off graciously. I didn't leave my place. They couldn't get me off balance with their slow hands and arms alone. So, Lilay had to try and shoulder check me to the ground.

I bounded back quickly. Slightly stopped on the pavement. That got me serious. I was no punk. I took a stance. The easiest one, and my favorite go to. Left fist up in a sideways guarding stance. Right arm across my chest, defensive and protective. Fightning Stance. If they wanted a fight, I'd give them a karate black belt's fight.

"Oh no!",

Atey mocked,

"she's gonna use her 'karate' powers on us!"

She tried doing exaggerated moves. Hooting and hollering like a cartoon character. Until she finally swung her real attack. I misread it as an open palm strike. She was trying to slap my head. But I blocked it smoothly like I have done so many times before. Stepped in. Gave her a full straight open palm into her gut just below her ribs. A diaphragm blow so she couldn't breathe. She spent the next minutes wheezing on the floor. She was right about those karate "powers".

"You're dead!"

Nashay shouted. She charged at me with her arms up and swung them down. These girls never fought anyone who wasn't scared. Or already on their hands and knees to protect themselves. It was their first real fight, and they lost hard. I did a standing roundhouse kick to her side and hit her ribs. She went down too.

That just left Lilay, who was on the defensive after what she had just saw. She came at me anyway, thinking her larger frame would somehow avoid what was waiting for her. I did a 360 Tiger Tail Ground Sweep. And before she even thought about what she would do to me when she grabbed me. She dropped hard right on her stomach and knees. I was standing right before she hit the ground. Her own momentum took her out with a simple ground sweep.

I stood by and waited for the girls to get themselves together. I wanted to see their defeated faces twisted in pain and regret. I wanted to hear them beg for forgiveness, so I could barter their pride with the weight of my fist.

I was impatient.

"Listen up,"

I declared.

"If you don't want me to actually *try seriously next* time, you better start doing what I say. If this school's going to have a leader, it's going to be me. Got it?"

Lilay turned to her sisters and their fear-stricken faces, and she nodded. I was the queen of the school from that point on. My fist was iron, cold, and of course, **Chilly**, just like me.

CHAPTER 4

My plan was simple, even for a 10-year-old. I wanted to rule the school. And when Nico came into the same system as me, I'd keep him pushed back. All the shame and loneliness I felt at home, I'd exact my revenge as the dominant queen of the school. There wasn't much of a plan after that. I was just angry. All I had was my strength. And my beauty, of course. If my Pa gave me my strength by enrolling me in karate for my own protection. Then my Mama gave me beauty by inheriting her good looks. It was a time before most boys were developed enough to understand their own feelings of attraction. But the environment was brutal. Kids were learning swear words before they finished learning simple math. The race for maturity started young for all of us.

Boys were lining up to talk to me. I was seen as the most interesting and prettiest girl in the whole school. I was pretty, and I still am; that much is true. But the most interesting was from a mixed bag of my own talents.

I had to stand out. School became the home away from home I needed. I aced every test, even cheated to do it. So that everyone would think I was the smartest. I was naturally athletic, yet I practiced my karate and kata forms every single day. This was as a form of self-improvement. Even though I never felt the effects until so much later. As a result, I was a gym star. Good at every game and could overcome every obstacle. People loved me because I was a winner. That's all my school ever taught me.

The last year before the aliens came — weeks before, as a matter of fact, I decided to flex my power in a real, dominant way. I organized a student beauty award. Girls would vote for the most handsome boy, and boys would vote for the prettiest girl. My goal was to get the best pick of all the boys approved by all the girls, and I already knew who that was. A boy named Orlando. He was all anyone could talk about. He was a winner and stood out with grace and charm, like how I tried my hardest to do.

What I wasn't expecting. Was competition. I had the Stacks girls as my enforcers to make sure no one was planning to run against me. To make sure no boys would be speaking out against me, either. At that point. I had already broken a lot of hearts. I took gifts without exchanging the same feelings. I spurned many "lovers" before any of us really knew what "loving" each other would be. There were jealous boys. They could have screwed up my chances.

In the end. The vote came to pass. Orlando won the vote easily. Almost no one voted for anyone else. Except the proud, outspoken girls who already had boyfriends and wanted to brag about it. Then came the reading of the ballots for the prettiest girl.

A girl named Heather won.

Some brown-haired country girl. Who moved in. Was nice as could be. Popular for her sincere kindness. Definitely not prettier than me. She won by a single vote without doing anything. The Stacks girls weren't even aware of her. None of us had her on our radar. No boy mentioned her. They all either lied or weren't intimidated enough to vote for me. She was just newer, mysterious and unknown.

That's all it took to defeat me?

That was the first real loss I ever counted. I set it up. I set the challenge. I put myself at risk, for honor and prestige, to win, and I failed. I failed even though I was stronger and had more opportunities. Even though I could have made her look hideous in one minute. I lost to her then. That loss hit me hard.

I felt like a loser. Inferior. Ugly. Discarded. Abandoned. All the same feelings I avoided at home came to roost at school too. The Stacks became the only girls who hung around me when the word got out that the whole contest was supposed to be rigged for me. Heather and Orlando started hanging out as a coincidence. It looked like they would start dating. My whole world was falling apart.

Again.

Then the aliens came. And somehow, even back then. For as smart as I was for a ten-year-old. I thought my own problems were more important. That was when I left for good. The whole world was ending, not just mine, but it felt like I wasn't part of that whole world event. I felt like I had to get away, or my hate and everyone's panic would just cause me to finally snap.

I still remember. The only one who knew I was leaving was Nico. He saw me off. Although, he didn't know it. I told him I'd be back.

"Your sissy is strong, and she's going to go fight the aliens off to leave us all alone."

"But what if they want to be our friends?"

Nico asked. He was only five at the time, still happy as could be, but he looked worried at that time. Not for himself, either. And not even for me. He cared more about the aliens that I could hurt if I actually did try and take them on. He was scared on their behalf. Scared of me for them. As he should.

And that hurt. It really did. I didn't think it would. I finally had superiority over him, a sure sign that I was stronger and better than him. But I couldn't enjoy it at all. Deep down, I was still that happy girl who loved her family, and I still am, but it's deep below a cold exterior. I have a body like a glacier now, cut and icy. The love in me is like a fly trapped in the core of thousands of tons of ice.

I went into Gibraltar on my own, years after my brother did, to find a place where I could hate in peace and privacy...

CHAPTER 5

Gibraltar accepted everyone, regardless of where you came from. They united all people with a single language that they beamed directly into people's brains. I wasn't into that. I could see the signs, and they revealed themselves more and more clearly as time went on. This wasn't a rescue effort; it was a containment plan.

For the next eight years, I was stuck in a program for lost and orphaned children. A surprising number of adults committed suicide as soon as the aliens landed. Or even a little before then, when the presence of their ship was detected. It wasn't a pandemic sort of deal. But it left many kids without families and in countries too flustered to raise them.

I was in a home with no love and full of kids that divided the attention of our caregivers. I was ignored and alone. Again. This time, it wasn't even my own fault. I got more violent and practiced my katas in secret. Hurting no one but myself through rigorous training. I was convinced it would help me someday. In this new alien world of uncertainty, I would need to be the strongest and the fastest alive no matter what. If we were being collected like animals, I wanted to be so important no one could replace or get rid of me. I wanted celebrity status, so I wouldn't be forgotten again. When I hit my teen years. When my body started growing faster. And my mind got more developed. I discovered Batey as it was still up and coming.

At that time. Other sports and activities distracted people from their harsh reality. They gladly dove right into it. I thought it was pathetic, and when I said as much, I got kicked out of their events. No one would practice with me as I was either too strong or too right for them to listen to.

The whole life I lived up until then felt like a lie. The spaceship was becoming the new normal. Which I knew was wrong to begin with. That's when I started noticing the real situation. Through everyone's smiles. I saw the reasons they had hidden deep inside themselves for trying to be happy. Without this. They had nothing. Without the ship, they just had a dying planet. And the ship had everything they ever wanted.

Even though I was still cold, being Chilly as best as I could be, I didn't start getting any Cred until I turned 18. I was also restricted to juvenile leagues only at that time, matched up with kids in my age and grade group. And I made them all look like chumps.

Eventually, I got to meet up with the Stacks sisters. Their whole family came aboard, and I didn't let them forget our arrangement. They all got fat and lazy, but they had connections. They weren't the enforcers I used to have, but that society was over and done with. Ruling people with the fear of power didn't hold their sway in the cities on the ship. Most crimes were stomped out by drones that scanned the streets constantly. Even if we got up to our old ways again, we'd get caught and punished for it.

We stayed in contact. I would find a use for them. Eventually. Until then, I had to keep myself busy, or the loneliness, and the abandonment, would have driven me insane. I would have been just like the Stacks, getting fat on rations. Lusting after pin-up model men and gearing myself up to be a part of the system that surrounded me.

I didn't go quietly, that's for sure. Every decision I made had a goal behind it. An objective that went unseen by those who watched me. I was determined to keep my silence and my peace. Just like hiding my katas, I hid my true intentions. That way, no one could counter them. If they learned how I fought, they'd know how to beat me. But if I kept my hands hidden until the final moment, they would be unprepared.

My first goal was in sight. Batey became a recognized premium sport. No more baseball, basketball or football. It was all about New Batey and the stars that played it. Now that I remember, that was the first time I ever saw Gorri, too. On a billboard, advertising the playoffs of the first-ever official game league.

When I turned 18, I was surprised to find just how much PCred I got by being good at the game. Ups from my teammates, respect from my defeated foes, courtesies that I never paid back. And I spent all that goodwill like it was rotting. I became targeted, hated, and despised by players from all over. They upgraded my nickname from Chilly to Ice Queen. Some even called me numb. And I felt that.

My whole life on Earth prepared me for a miserable run of things. For a life of suffering under my own bad decisions made out of hatred. After dipping my toes into that icy water, I was ready to accept that, but the aliens came and everything changed. They changed by being forced to remain the same. Just as I was ready to change myself again. From Happy to Chilly.

And hopefully off to something different. The world changed and forced me to stay the same to compensate.

New Batey started my life over, while I was still suffering from the wounds of my old one. If I weren't so cold, I could have loved it, enjoyed it, smiled about it and been happy just to play it. I was good at it, and when I played, I never lost. My team did, but not me. It made me feel like I belonged again, like I was wanted. But then all that changed, because change is always happening. No matter how much we try to keep things the same.

CHAPTER 6

When I was 18, I hit the first real problem of my life. It wasn't just a loss; it was way worse. It was something I could never have prepared for. Even now, it's like a scar inside my heart. It's a memory of when I realized that life changes, people don't, and no matter what, you'll always be who you used to be. It's what made me Chilly again, on the outside and deep within.

I won a game against a hastily assembled team on the promise of a quick Cred match. We were all pathetic, and I was arguably the worst off that day, but they didn't care. They wanted to test me, failed my test, and complained about things not being fair. I had to agree with them. Things weren't fair. Because some people in the world, or on the ship, have to face off with me, which means they lose. Even on my off days, I am still leagues above others.

They didn't take that easily. They followed me home, so I turned away. I tried to stay on the streets, but they surrounded me one by one. I had to run into an alley built between residences. Everyone knew the windows were for show and wouldn't open. And no one would hear me scream if something happened to me.

They tried. I beat two of them up with some quick sidekicks and a barrage of round house kicks to the nose. Then I got grabbed from behind by an unseen third. I tried to kick myself free, but the one whose nose I broke, he grabbed my legs and reached up to my waist to tear my clothes off. I didn't give them an inch. I struggled the whole way through, even though I couldn't beat them. Even if they did **it.** I swore. I wouldn't lose.

But they didn't. Someone else showed up at the last moment and chased them off. A man saving my life was the last thing I wanted. Or needed. I was ready to hate him outright. To tear him down and shave years off his life with the sound of my voice. But I couldn't. Because I lost to him.

I lost to his eyes that were like glistening rounded gems of glass off the rim of a broken bottle. I lost to his husky, deep voice like the hull of the ship creaking from construction in the distance. I lost to his smokey, brown skin and his thick, black beard that didn't quite hide enough of his rock-solid jawline.

I lost to love. I didn't even try to fight back. I was in love from that moment on, and I showed it in the worst way possible. I tried to fight him for my honor back, but I couldn't put my all into it, no matter how much I tried. He handled me, swung me around. He was good, and as much as I wanted to say that I was better, I couldn't. I had never had a loss like that before in my life. But there it was, staring me down. I couldn't beat this guy. He was handsome and charming and saved me from the lowest point I have ever been in.

It wasn't like before. Orlando was a status symbol to me. I recognized that he was handsome, but that was just a tool for me to use. He was pretty because I should have gotten him in the end and been together with him as a power couple in school. There was a reason, a hard, *cold*, logic behind why I found that boy attractive. My heart wasn't giving me any reasons to fall for this guy, though. His name was Levitate, and that's exactly how my heart rate felt with him.

And what's worse is that I enjoyed it. Not because I wanted to be alone or keep myself distant. I was tired of being cold every day, tired of being Chilly, but that's all I knew at that point. I hadn't changed. I was trying to when the aliens came. It was their fault, not mine. Anyone's fault but mine, that I fell in love.

We stayed together for a while, didn't get married, and fooled around for a while. He took care of me, and I took care of him. He was the first man in my life. The first man I recognized was stronger than me. Someone I could depend on. I wanted to give him everything for that. I wanted him to melt me down and start me new.

But I got pregnant.

I was scared at first, remembering my own childhood. I reminded myself that things are different now. No one was starving or left wanting; there was always stuff to do, there was no food shortage. For one, I thought well of the aliens ruling over us. And when I told Levitate, he vanished, and I never saw him again. My face and my heart was fated to never have happiness for long.

I had a decision to make. Alone, what good was I? What kind of mother would I be for a child that represented a whole new chapter of my life of hate? What would I do to this tiny life if it was left with me for too long? I wouldn't get postpartum depression; I'd go full postpartum rage. Thinking of a small little child like I used to be, they'd probably be happy all the time, even if I never loved them. They'd get by with a smile anywhere in the world or on the spaceship.

And I couldn't kill a child. Of any size, from anywhere. Not by myself or with help. So I rode it out and had the baby. When it was stable enough to leave the medical center in Gibraltar. I did what I could to use as much of my PCred as I had earned from all the games I'd played. Even the pity money given for my circumstances, and I left my son up for adoption with the top childcare center. No foster homes, no orphanages. A straight shot to the best of the best who were looking to adopt a healthy human boy.

They could have him and give him everything I couldn't. Love. Time. And undivided attention. A happy child had no place in my cold world. From then on, I was committed to only one person. I'd be alone until I died. And then, I'd be truly happy.

I always had myself.

CHAPTER 7

New Batey kept taking off. For the next three years, I was merciless at the game. I went all over, played in every district, every sector. I never stayed in one place too long. I'd travel, enroll, win, and leave. Every win was a record for me, and every loss was a new enemy I made. A new rival. Or a new grudge.

Zero teams kept me past the preliminary phases. I didn't understand why. I was the best player, no doubt, every time. I played every position with an unstoppable presence. I occupied the playing field. I was twice as fast as rival teams and never took a penalty without taking someone down with me. But they hated me. Because I was too cold with it. They were all jealous, as they should be.

Half the teams treated each other like a family, and it made me sick. The other half, wasn't worth bothering with. They were bad, and they didn't care. They seemed to like their own mediocrity and couldn't be asked to try as hard as me. And when I tried to drill a sense of winning in them, they said I was too "rough". So I started leaving early to make sure they wouldn't hound me.

Being disliked and even hated for being too good was just the kind of life I was hoping to live out. It kept me cold and kept other people away. Or it would have if I hadn't met "him." One day in a far-off sector, I played a game outside of the facility where New Batey was developed. A testing lab for new Sphere fields. It was a net pay job, and I'd get more PCred for doing it than NCred for when I walked away from my teams with bad impressions.

The other team was good. In particular, one stood out. He was an older guy, in his 40s or something, at least that's what it appeared like, and he was a leader. He commanded the whole team from the back, barely moved, and when he did, it was a power play. He was an all-rounder and focused on winning. That's why he got so hot and bothered when he lost to me.

After the match, he lectured his team. Even though it was just a test. He broke them down like they were professionals that just lost an exhibition match. They thought it didn't matter.

"Well, it did matter,"

he vocalized,

"because these fields expect the best of the best to be in them, and you're up there playing like you're falling asleep!"

I respected him, at least a little, when he said that. He was making a lot of sense and making it known with a thunderous voice. But I stayed too long and unfortunately, caught his eye. The worst thing about a man like him. A real macho. Do everything. Patriarch type, is how he thinks his respect is something sacred. That once earned, has put you in a place in his life you can't escape from. And he came up to me with some words of praise that I could have done without.

"You do karate?"

he questioned. I didn't answer, but he didn't need one. He was talking at me, not to me.

"I could tell. Your stances, the way you controlled your court. I'm a former half-dan at judo, so I know a few things about implementing martial arts into New Batey. It's half of what the game was designed to accommodate, and it's perfect for players like you."

"Well... I **am** good,"

I muttered. I tried to leave like that was it. My own thank you for recognizing me, so he could feel good about himself after, but no, not this man. Not Gorri. He saw potential, which I already knew I had, but he felt like it was his duty to remind me about it.

"You need to sign onto a professional team,"

he emphasized.

"Every day you're not on one; you're wasting your talents."

His first impression was to mansplain and cajole me into following his way of life. His guideline for success. His plan. Not mine. He thought I would be happier that way. Well. The last man I followed made me the unhappiest I'd ever been. I had good reason to suspect an older one would find new ways to piss me off.

But Gorri didn't give up. He saw me leaving and followed me, talking about sports training this. Founding the sport that. A lot of stuff I heard over again later, that I ignored the first time. But I made it clear I had no interest in listening to him. I punched him in the chest and knocked him over. But to his credit, he recovered immediately, rolled backward and was on his feet the next second.

"That's a foul,"

he explained.

"No hand or foot contact. Maybe in the minor or off leagues, but in the official circuit? No way. You have to learn to fight with your elbows and knees. Have you heard of Silat or Muy Thai?"

"No,"

I retorted. I tried to leave again, but he kept following me. He basically chased me. I got away for a moment, went to another sector, and he found me there too. I tried laying low for a while, but every time I resurfaced to play Batey, he was there and calling me out. He criticized my plays. Heckled me between rounds. When my team would lose, he blamed it on me.

When I didn't see him, I ended up playing worse. When I played, all I could focus on was body checking and fighting in the field. But that's what he praised me for the most. He liked watching me fight.

"Women should follow a man's lead,"

he declareed more than once.

"If a woman's stronger than a man, it's because she's trying to find a man strong enough to take her down."

I hated Gorri.

Somehow, it wasn't the right kind of hate, and it wasn't painful or hurting. All the other hate I felt made me feel hot inside and made my exterior colder to keep it all in. This hate made me feel cold, giving me chills as I had lived through it once. I never admitted it, but I once thought maybe he was right...

CHAPTER 8

When I was 23. I finally had enough of everything. The world around me was a prison camp where we were all dancing and flying around with our toys. Pretending to be happy, while a bunch of faceless blue tubes with "hands" controlled our fate. They were spectators, and the Earth was their fireworks show and we were their zoo. They just wanted to see things go down and didn't care that we had thoughts and feelings. They let us suffer for, what it felt like, I'd never know. Time felt different in the spaceship.

And Gorri wouldn't shut the hell up. I had to get him off my back for good, so I challenged him. His team against me. Five on one, and I'd still kick their asses. I meant it, too. It wasn't just a hot-headed brag; it was a threat because I'd done it before. I played in games where my teammates were detriments, straight up working against me, a 1v9, and I still won. They lost, but I could make goals, I could send them out of the sphere, and I could get things done that they couldn't.

So I went for it. I tried them. The Absolutes were their name, and it was an all-male racket. A scrawny little boy named Tyger, wearing stripes he didn't earn. A masked up cyborg named IND23, same as the serial number on his face, giving up his identity for God knows why. A fella named Black. Who tagged the Absolute title to his name, is more of a pin-up magazine boy than a real combat sport type. And of course, Gorri, the coach and "part-time" member, since he was recruiting me for a while.

"There's only four of you,"

I reported.

"And you have your own logo and lockers?"

"We absolutely do,"

Black proclaimed. He was dumb and thought that pun hit. I actually liked his goofy demeanor.

"We lost a member,"

Tyger divulged,

"from an injury. A field malfunction occurred, and he quit during his treatment. We haven't heard back from him in, uh....a year, so we're pretty sure he's not coming back."

He was like a little kid. In fact, he couldn't have been old enough to be from Earth properly. He could have been born up here or born and then brought up right after. A sad, tiny boy.
"Well,"
I stated,

"I'm not about to abuse a team that can't even play. Sorry, but you lost before this began."

"We do have five members,"

IND23 chimed. I turned for clarification. But what I hate the most about this future land is how it took away all our humanity without asking for it first. Men like him. For whatever reason. Could just change around the parts of their bodies and become something new. Not human enough, in my opinion. I couldn't read his face, so I didn't want to look at it.

"I guess it's time to come clean,"

Gorri confessed.

"I did promise you'd be fighting my team, and you did clarify that there would be five of us against one of you. However. I thought about it. The way you phrased that challenge. Officially, it doesn't preclude you from also being a part of the team you were facing."

"What are you talking about?!"

I demanded. I wasn't expecting what happened next. He pulled out a contract with my signature on it. Something I must have signed a long time ago and forgotten about. It was the sign-up flyer for the test where Gorri and I met. Four years ago, and he still had it, and I figured out why.

"You already joined my team,"

he afirmed.

"I changed the name over the years, but they've remained Absolutely in my management."

"Abso-LUTE-ly,"
Black echoed back, the hype man that he was.

"The sign-up sheets,"

he explained,

"were for permissions and privileges associated with the team I formed. Who used the Sphere field under provisional practice license. At that time, our team had ten members, including me and including you. The match we played back then was for sparring."

"You lying, tricking.....mansplaining, piece of -!",

I clamored.

"Woah, easy there,"

he pronounced.

"Let's not say something we would regret."

He started to put the document away, and I snapped. I moved in with my fists up, full aggression, no defense in my stance. Tyger dove away, and I thought I was dealing with a team that was all show. But then they moved. IND23 countered me and caught my fist with his forearm. I punched solid bone through muscle. Black stood in my way, so I kicked him in the sternum, but he took it and held his ground.

"You can't fight like that,"

Black warned. It was like the pain didn't reach his brain yet. I ignored IND23 and ducked in for another punch at Black's gut. Same place, right under the ribs. A diaphragm shot that won so many fights. I took IND23's knee to my stomach first and only tapped Black's skin before getting kicked back. I recovered with a roll and stood up in defense.

"Elbows and knees,"

IND23 instructed.

"That's what I told her,"

Gorri advised,

"and she wouldn't believe me. She's got good moves for a ground fighter, but her game in the air is as sloppy as they come. Just downright -."

"You're strong,"

IND23 annouced. The first right thing I heard that whole day.

"If you join us, you can get stronger."

"Why would I need to do that?"

I asked. I didn't believe them. I was tricked into joining their team. Filling their gap. Fixing their mistakes, and they were fighting me over it. I didn't want to do what other people told me. To change for them and not for myself.

"Because you can get stronger,"

he informed.

"And then you can help yourself."

I felt the same melting feeling from before, and for a man without a face. My fear, and an aching loss in my lower abdomen, made me feel weak. That's how I joined the Absolutes. They convinced me that I had no choice. Those things could never be the same. I had to change, and be changed, to be happy.

Great. What I feared the most.

CHAPTER 9

Two years went by. Years of off-league matches. Minor league incidents and the first steps to a full league sponsored match. But we still didn't have a real fifth. In that time, I did change. I stayed Chilly, the Ice Queen of the Sphere Field, but I was someone else, too. I wasn't opening up like a family, but I was respecting them like real teammates.

But Tyger was still pathetic. He got worse over two years. He was good at social management. Getting PCred from our matches. Upgrading our gear as sponsorships and convincing a cheer squad to stand by for our goals. Every time I slammed one in, they shivered like they got hit with a winter wind up their skirts. I thought it was annoying and exploitative at first, and I still think that now, but it's not all about me. It's about making the other team feel bad for my success.

That's what changed the most. I started to think that it was not about me. I was only thinking of myself when I gave up my kid, but any old orphanage would have done the job if that was the truth. I didn't need to change out all the PCred I ever gathered to give that kid a chance at a better life. I could have left him on the street, and a drone would have picked him up. But it wasn't about me.

I got to thinking. Real hard, how much of my life was I making all about me, and how much of that part of my life led me to suffer because of it? How many times was I wrong to think that way and act that way? If I were still alone by then, I never would have considered it. I never would have changed for the better.

But it still wasn't quite enough. I still hated Gorri, but it developed into a more fatherly kind of hate. I hated him insisting his way of life on me, but I didn't hate him as a coach or fellow player. And he knew that and tried to stop, but he never really could. He'd go silent for a few days. No advice. No contact except for training, and then all of a sudden.

> "Hey Chilly. Why don't we run perimeter drills so you
> can avoid the scrim fights. And sneak around to the
> goal line for surprise plays?"

Trying to keep me out of the place where men were supposed to fight. Because I was keeping up with them, and his poor old heart couldn't take it.

Black stayed the same, and I was happy that he never changed. He's the perfect kind of man for a woman like me. He's full of himself, charmless, arrogant, bold and stupid. The only problem is. He's also all of those things, self-obsessed, and believes he's doing a favor to anyone he looks at with a smile. And the problem is. Most of them react that way because he's just as loveable in short bursts as he is hateable in constant contact.

IND23 was my real rival, of sorts. He pushed me to be better, but I never let him admit he was stronger. He had enhancements. Without those, he'd be beneath me.

"I was totally blind: nearsighted, astigmatic and with cataracts. This is my upgrade for vision,"

he admitted.

"Yeah, you'd be weaker than me,"

I reiterated.

"I suppose so,"

he confessed.

"And if I had no internal organs, you'd also be better at taking dumps in the toilet than me."

"A win is a win,"
I confirmed. He never got agitated, which somehow just made me feel worse. I was pushing him away because it felt natural. A man liking me was a disaster waiting to happen for both of us, so I had to keep them all away as much as possible. I never wanted to make the mistake of loving someone again.

We heard there was a young talent rising up. He was getting scouted all over and looking for a place to stay. Another sucker into the mix. Another loser who lost his mind and tried to make things the same again. Embracing change for the wrong reasons. When I heard he was on his way here, I was ready to reject him outright if he couldn't keep up with me.

One day as I was going to the team meeting, and I heard a commotion in our small practice facility. As I walked in, I saw a familiar face lying on the ground. He quickly scrambled to get up to present himself.

"What's going on here?"

I questioned, puzzled at who this could be.

"This is our new teammate, Nico Pengin,"

Gorri proclaimed, proud and matter of fact.

Those words cracked me open. The glacier that was my wall, it shattered like fake glass on a movie set. I couldn't believe it, but it was true. I could still see that happy boy in his face when he smiled. The one I tried to hurt, the one I hated, the one that sent me running away, and in the end, still admired me. And when we met for the first time, for real, as brother and sister again, I felt 10 years old.

I was smiling a little bit and shed a tear, but I couldn't fix myself up. I was all open. I wasn't Chilly anymore. What made me the happiest was that he was still himself. He hadn't changed. He grew. He was who he was, he never changed, but he made himself better, where I ended up becoming worse the longer I was alone. I felt like crying until I puked.

But that's what he almost did instead. He was so glad to see me. And I couldn't think of anything to say back.

"Your sissy's still strong,"

I recited after awhile.

"Now, we can fight together."

At least he didn't take me seriously. He thought I was talking about playing Batey together.

But there's still more to it than that....

CHAPTER 10

After the playoff match. We were literal celebrities, and celebrities got followed to their homes. Luckily. After years of dealing with Gorri's nonsense. I got good at avoiding the reporters seeking Cred of their own and slipped away from the crowd. I had something important to do, and no one could find out.

I got inside my home. Which was in the center of the sector—a nice high-rise apartment for a high rising celebrity like me. A report about our game, and Nico's rule-bending maneuver, was on the viewfinder. I turned it off. I was there, I had already seen it, and I knew how important it could be. Those Flash Flight boots were strong, and they could probably outrace a police drone.

I had a call to make, and not a normal one. I needed the monitor for it. And some other things lying around. My apartment looks messy because it is, but everything is where it is because I always need it. Just in case I need to talk to someone.

Someone in the Returnance.

I connected to my private network. Set up in secret to allow us to communicate. A secure line that even the Blues don't know about. And can never find out about no matter what. Modifying their tech was illegal and dangerous, but some knew how, and they shared the same goals.

I'd never talk about this with the team, especially not Nico. Not unless I had to save his life. I spent so long thinking for myself. Acting for myself, and not knowing how important my family really was, how thankless I had been. If it came to, and the chance came up, I'd include him, but only him.

The monitor flickered a few times before it got the signal. All the wires I put into it. Into all the confusing ports from the space where it was built into the wall. It let me talk to people in their own stations, all hidden and undercover just like me. This time, however, it led me to the Stacks sisters. Atey, Nashay and Lilay, my confidantes, my crew. They helped me set everything up. They found the help we needed. They even made the connections with their own work above the line. All while I was gathering the Cred and popularity to keep their work in the dark.

"What's the daily sitrep?"

I requested.
Atey spoke first.

"We found a major ally,"

she affirmed.

"Someone who works near the mothership's main docking port. Where they send their smaller ships out on probing missions. It's a restricted, privileged area, but he thinks he can run some wires down there to hook us up. As a forward operating base."

"Good,"

I declare.

"But how can we pilot their ships?"

Nashay answered,"

"It's not their ships we'll be piloting. While we could sustain ourselves in their craft, we can't land them on the planet. They're too dense and would sink into the ground no matter where we put them. That's why they have to use the retractor beams to pull people up."

"We can lower them down,"

I proposed.

"We'll find a way to dock them somehow if we need to. Or just let them have them back and scrap the retractor beams inside for our own use."

"We could,"

Atey uttured.

"But once we're on Earth, as long as they're still here, they could just come and take it back."

Not unless we sent them a couple of nuclear warheads or something, I would bet. Those thoughts stayed inside. No matter how secure our connection was. No matter how evasive we were about our plans. There was always the chance that someone could hear us and give us hell for it.

Lilay had the most to say and said it last.

"I looked into something more personal for you, Chilly,"

she began.

"You remember about seven years ago, where you were in life?"

"You're not far enough away from me that I can't kick your ass if you make me remember,"

I threatened.

"I'm not about to insult you,"

she contested,

"but please stay calm. This is important; it could be an out for us. A way into the Pathing Program."

The piloting institute. Training cadets. From as young as birth. To telekinetically control alien technology with their thoughts. Psychic supergenius child pilots for deep space activities. The farming labor portion of the zoo. If all of us were just meant to entertain the aliens, what excuse did they have to keep us alive at their expense?

The first generation would die out. And the replacements would know nothing about the Earth. Those born in space would be subjugated by it. They'd be born not knowing freedom or any culture but the culture the Blues create. And what future do they have in mind for humanity? According to the Pathing Institute, it's either forced labor or war. They want to raise us like animals and make us do their work. Cultivate us. Domesticate us with sports and leisure, then mold us into their own better image.

"What's the way in?"

I inquired. Lilay sighed. She sounded pitiable and shaken by the news she was about to deliver. No, she was pitying me. Somehow, deep in my gut, I knew it.

"They match DNA samples for candidates. But they change the names and sometimes the appearances of certain cadets. To help them fit into the environment better. It's a whole different world in there. Where they turn ordinary human children into alien hybrid geniuses. At this point. A seven-year-old child would have the equatable mind of a late teenager, or possibly an early adult."

"What are you saying?"

I had to ask to get to the point. I forced the truth out of her, just like we planned to force the truth out of Gibraltar itself.

"We found traces of your offspring. His name is Ashy Arden,"

Lilay whispered.

"He was at the game this afternoon, I believe in the Absolutes. He attended with his adopted father, who oversaw the match in special accommodations. His adopted father is the Pathing Program co-director, Dr. Juracán."

"*That* Dr. Juracán!?"

Atey exclaimed.

So it was true. In my heart, I felt it, the beat of another further down. My son was there. Transformed. And adopted by the most powerful. Highly-credited alien tech scientist, in what became our captive prison world. Not just that, but he has been so close to me this entire time?!?! My mind cannot comprehend all these mixed emotions... How am I supposed to act around him now? My own flesh and blood... Do I tell Nico Pengin? Or the team? Do I tell Arden how much power resides within him? Not because of anything special, other than because of who adopted him.

Because if Arden, my son, does what is needed, he could lead us all to freedom....

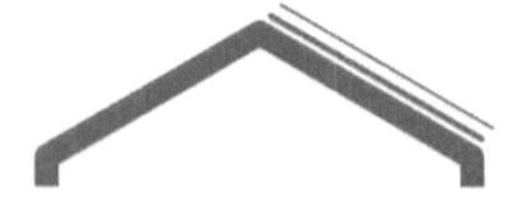

What Did You Think of Batey Descending?

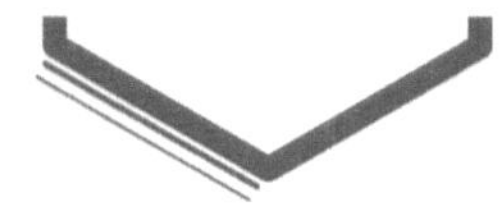

First of all, thank you for purchasing this book. I know you could have picked any number of books to read, but you picked this book, and I am extremely grateful for that.

I hope that it adds value and quality to your everyday life. If so, it would be really nice if you could share this book with your friends and family by posting it on Facebook[1] and Twitter[2].

If you enjoyed this book and found some benefit in reading this, I'd like to hear from you and hope that you could take some time to post a review where you acquired the book. Your feedback and support will help me to greatly improve my writing craft for future projects and make the next book even better.

I want **you**, the **reader**, to know that your **review** is very important to me as an **author**. If you are able to **leave a review**, please be sure to leave one as soon as you are able to do so, at the retailer you acquired this book. Every single review is **instrumental** in my journey as an author, and I hope you are able to help me with this request of **your opinion**. (Examples: Was the book **too long, too short, too graphic**, not enough **development**, would you like

---

1. https://www.facebook.com/

2. https://twitter.com/?lang=en

to see more of **certain characters** or did you **enjoy the story?** The **sports action?** The **drama?** The **back** and **forth** from the **present day story to the past?**). Thank you for reading here thus far on my selfish requests, I wish you the best in your future success!

And if you would like to read the first book in the series, Batey Ascending, is available on the same retail platforms as Batey Descending.

Don't miss out!

Visit the website below and you can sign up to receive emails whenever Nico Pengin publishes a new book. There's no charge and no obligation.

https://books2read.com/r/B-A-UAQN-JMURB

BOOKS 2 READ

Connecting independent readers to independent writers.

Did you love *Batey Descending*? Then you should read *Batey Ascending*[3] by Nico Pengin!

Inspired by Alita: Battle Angel, Harry Potter's Quidditch game and the Tainos of the Caribbean.

A family oriented, space, futuristic sport, where family is involved. Based on a Native American sport from the Taino people of the Dominican Republic and imagined futuristic technology. Futuristic jetpacks but on boots, with aerial hacky sack/soccer and an antigravity ball. The objective is to score in the opponents floating ring/goal. You will need to have an imagination in order to get into this future. Because it could

<hr>

3. https://books2read.com/u/31K8Mv

4. https://books2read.com/u/31K8Mv

happen, as humans naturally destroy the Earth, being bad caretakers of it. If we were capable of creating this technology with assistance from benevolent extraterrestrials. Who are bored in space and decide to save willing humans on their massive ship. Then it's a possibility, as we would give them entertainment with a new sport in a new environment.

As seen on Goodreads:"Batey Ascending is a unique science fiction novel about a sports event that is popular in a dystopian future. Nico, the main character, has had the chance to escape the Earth before it was destroyed and now is one of the main athletes of a new and risky sport. Drama, suspense and action are present throughout Nico's adventure.I really liked the plot and how it was written. The author, Nico Pengin, has done a marvellous job in describing this new world in a realistic and riveting way. I was fully captivated from the very beginning. Strongly recommended for teenagers and adults as well. 5 stars!-Carol M.

As seen in Amazon Reviews:"I am a diehard Science Fiction fan, with a mild interest in sports. When looking for a short read I came across Batey Ascending and decided to give it a go.

Am I ever happy I did! Five stars across the board and a new author on my watch list.

Nico is one of the millions of humans who took up the Alien's amazing offer of refuge on their giant space ship. Earth was about to implode.

All the humans were treated equally ... a space to live in, and all the basic necessities. After several years of settling in, it became apparent that entertainment was missing and thus the ancient sport of Batey was revived and re-invented to work in a no gravity environment.

Nico decided to give it a try ... got hooked as was now working on "pro" status.

The competition is enhanced cyborgs and genetically modified humans.

The question is, can a ragtag group of humans even begin to compete?

This story line completes itself in this story, and leaves room for MORE! I'd love to see the MORE.

The Sci Fi Story: This honking big space ship shows up in Earth's orbit to witness its demise. The advanced technology aliens take pity on the humans and offer refuge.

They provide living accommodations, all necessities and actually allow humans access to their own technologies.

Though the world-building set up was there to support the futuristic Batey sports story, it really caught my interest.

I suspect that these aliens, who they are, where they came from and their technology could lead to the creation of a never ending series with the capability to take off in dozens of interesting directions and story lines.

I really enjoyed the story and am now waiting for MORE.

A highly recommended read. "-Vision Quest

" 'Lead strong to belong' - story leads you into the future " - Emmanuel

Read more at https://nicopengin.com/.

Also by Nico Pengin

Batey
Batey Ascending
Batey Descending

Batey - Español
Batey Ascendiendo

Standalone
la Insurrección de los Lápices
Uprising of the Pencils: Revised Edition
Batey

Watch for more at https://nicopengin.com/.

About the Author

Nico Pengin is a speculative fiction author who loves to create fun and imaginative stories that inspire kids and teens alike with a life-long love of reading. Drawing inspiration from his rich heritage as part of the Tainos people from the Caribbean, Nico Pengin is passionate about sharing his wild imagination with his readers. As an avid reader from a young age, he has been heavily inspired by books including Redwall by the late and great Brian Jacques, as well as Eiichiro Oda's manga, One Piece. Nico Pengin is currently working on a book series, and his comic called Batey. In his spare time, he enjoys working out, spending time with his supportive family, and living his life to the fullest. About the name Nico Pengin: Nico Pengin is a gamer tag designed to honor a friend and mentor of the author who served as a positive role model when he was younger. It also combines elements of the popular children's game Club Penguin, and the name has stuck with him ever since.

Read more at https://nicopengin.com/.

www.ingramcontent.com/pod-product-compliance
Lightning Source LLC
Chambersburg PA
CBHW031425160726
47993CB00003B/1398